LIFEVIEWS

Published by Creative Education
123 South Broad Street, Mankato, Minnesota 56001
Creative Education is an imprint of The Creative Company

Art direction by Rita Marshall; Production design by The Design Lab

Photographs by Georgienne Bradley and Jay Ireland

Library of Congress Cataloging-in-Publication Data

George, Michael.
Coral reefs / by Michael George.
p. cm. — (LifeViews)
Summary: Describes the different types of coral reefs and the creatures that live in them. Includes related activities.
Includes bibliographical references.
ISBN 1-58341-254-9
1. Coral reefs and islands—Juvenile literature. [1. Coral reefs and islands.] I. Title. II. Series.
QH95.8 .G46                          2003
577.7'89—dc21                        2002034785

First Edition

2  4  6  8  9  7  5  3  1

# CITIES OF THE SEA

# CORAL REEFS

### MICHAEL GEORGE

*Photographs by Georgienne Bradley and Jay Ireland*

# HUMAN BEINGS ARE

designed for life on land. As a result, many of us are somewhat biased. We feel that Earth's continents and islands are the most comfortable and beautiful places to live. But dry land is the exception on Earth—most of our planet is covered by **water**. Earth's blanket of water hides a world filled with unique sights, sounds, and beauty.

One of the most fascinating habitats beneath the ocean's surface is the **coral reef**. Located in warm, shallow seas, coral reefs are enormous, rocklike structures that are inhabited by peculiar forms of life. Underwater channels, crevices, and caves provide hiding

Oceans cover more than 70 percent of Earth's surface.

places for eels and sharks, octopuses and snails, odd-looking fish, and more microscopic **organisms** than a person could ever count. The coral reef is one of the most amazing collections of life in the world.

A coral reef is not formed in the same way that continents or islands are formed. Unlike mountains, deserts, and most other natural landscapes, it does not even consist of rocks and soil. Instead, it is a huge city built by tiny animals called **coral polyps**.

The construction of a coral reef is begun by a single coral polyp. Early in life, immature polyps, called planulae, drift freely through the ocean. Planulae are tiny, vulnerable animals; many are eaten by other sea creatures before they reach adulthood. Those that survive settle on the seafloor in shallow water. Here, the planulae develop into adult coral polyps.

Compared to creatures that are more familiar to us, such as dogs or humans, coral polyps are very simple animals. Even after they are fully grown, most coral polyps are smaller than

More than 500 coral species provide food and shelter for thousands and thousands of sea creatures around the world. Crabs (bottom), shrimp, sea stars, and fish are just a few of the animals that depend upon coral reefs for survival.

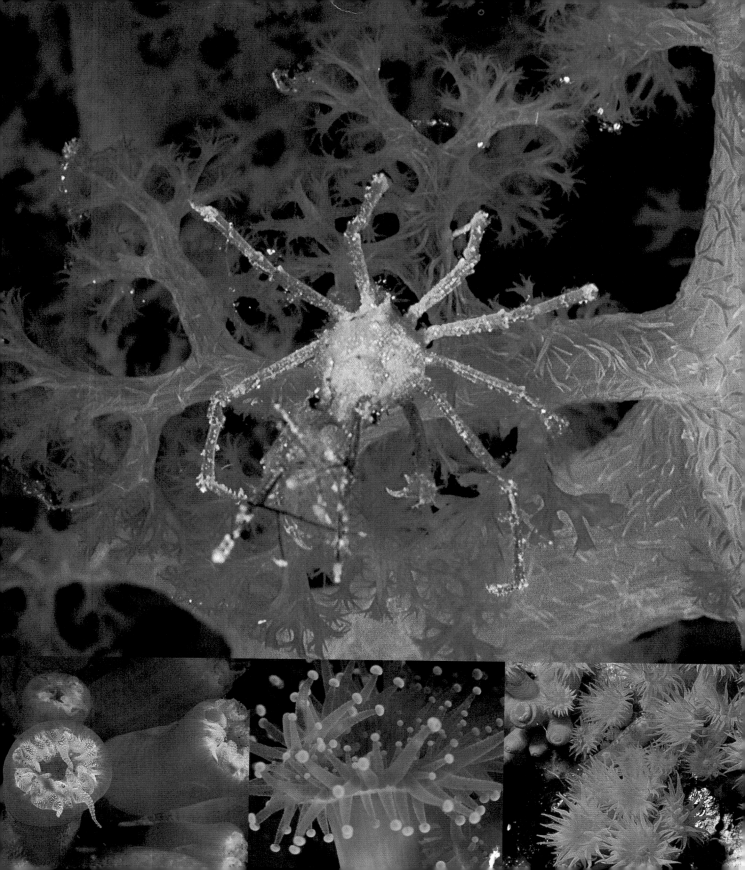

shelters remain. Given enough time, a new coral colony establishes itself upon the durable skeletons of its ancestors. Thus, over many hundreds of years, countless **generations** of polyps slowly produce a jumble of limestone boulders, branches, and shelves—a coral reef.

Coral reefs do not arise just anywhere beneath the ocean's surface. In order to develop properly, coral polyps have certain requirements. Reef-building polyps need **sunlight** to survive, so they cannot live in deep, dark ocean water. They also need warm water, abundant food, and fixed levels of salt and oxygen. The only places on Earth where all of these conditions are met are in **tropical** regions. As a result, living coral reefs are found only in clear, shallow water near Earth's equator.

Because reef-building polyps must live in shallow water, most coral reefs are located near land. Fringing reefs and barrier reefs are two common types of coral reefs. Fringing reefs are located directly off the shores of tropical islands and continents, whereas barrier reefs are separated from the shore by narrow stretches of calm, shallow water. The largest coral

Many corals grow quite fast, adding several inches per year.

reef in the world is a barrier reef. This enormous collection of coral, called the **Great Barrier Reef**, stretches for more than 1,200 miles (1,932 km) along the coast of Australia. It is the world's largest structure built by organisms, including humans.

**Atolls**, the third major type of coral reef, are isolated rings of coral. Unlike other reefs, atolls are usually located far from land, surrounded by nothing but water. Since coral polyps cannot survive in deep water, those isolated rings of coral puzzled scientists for many years. We now know that atolls are formed over thousands of years, as volcanic islands slowly sink beneath the surface of the ocean. The coral polyps grow fast enough to keep the top layer of the reef near the ocean's surface. Given enough time, some atolls develop into islands made entirely of coral.

As we have learned, fringing reefs, barrier reefs, and atolls are all constructed by stony corals. Stony corals, however, are not the only type of coral found in a reef. **Soft corals**, so named because they do not produce hard skeletons, also inhabit

The clear, warm, shallow waters off the shores of Palawan (opposite), an island in the Philippines, are ideal for fringing reef growth. Most reef-building corals prefer waters that are warmer than 64 °F (18 °C) on average.

many reefs. Because they are not supported by hard skeletons, soft coral colonies are much smaller and more delicate than stony coral colonies. Also unlike stony corals, soft corals do not need sunlight in order to develop properly. As a result, their colonies are often found in deeper parts of a reef.

Gorgonians are another type of coral living in many reefs. Like soft corals, gorgonian polyps lack hard, outer skeletons; however, they do have flexible internal skeletons. This enables their colonies to develop long, thin branches that look like delicate fans or feathers.

Coral polyps are not the only animals that live in coral reefs; thousands of other animals are nestled in the underwater cracks and crevices. One of the more interesting reef inhabitants is the **tube worm**. Tube worms do not look at all like the long, slithery worms that live on land. Many tube worms are decorated with thin tentacles that resemble flowers or delicate feather dusters. They use their tentacles to filter food from the water and to take in oxygen. Like coral polyps, tube worms withdraw into hard, rocklike shelters if they are disturbed.

Corals are the only organisms on Earth that can be seen from space. Orbiting spacecraft have photographed the Great Barrier Reef, comprised of countless stony corals, such as the staghorn (top), and soft coral colonies.

Butterflyfish have long snouts that they use to probe under-water cracks and crevices, where they can find tasty crabs and worms. Nurse sharks, on the other hand, do not need long snouts to capture hidden morsels of food. They move close to holes in the reef and suck up their victims like underwater vacuum cleaners.

The **moray eel**, another species of fish, is one of the most vicious-looking inhabitants of the coral reef. This snakelike fish hides from its victims in underwater caves. When an unsuspecting creature swims within reach, the eel lunges from its hiding place and snatches its victim in its sharp, pointed teeth.

The **wrasse** is a reef-dwelling fish that has one of the most unusual methods of acquiring food. This fish actually provides a cleaning service for other sea creatures. Using its long, pointed snout, the wrasse removes bits of debris from other fishes' bodies. It even picks up scraps of food from the teeth of sharks or eels. The arrangement works well for both parties—the wrasse gets bits of food to eat, while its customers receive a good cleaning.

Averaging three to six feet (1–2 m) in length and equipped with razor-sharp teeth, moray eels are one of the most ferocious predators of the coral reef. Fishes and crustaceans are their favorite prey.

While many reef animals have unusual methods for obtaining food, others simply rely on strength and speed. The great **barracuda**, often referred to as the "tiger of the sea," is always on the prowl for another meal. Growing up to 10 feet (3 m) long, an adult barracuda swims quietly through warm, tropical reefs. When an appetizing meal strays within range, the barracuda strikes with lightning-quick speed. Armed with powerful jaws filled with daggerlike teeth, the barracuda devours its meal with a few quick, clean bites.

Coral reefs are enormous cities hidden beneath Earth's tropical seas. They are built by tiny coral polyps and inhabited by millions of fascinating creatures. Coral reefs are unlike anything on land. Although we are only visitors, we are fortunate to get a glimpse of these underwater worlds and their amazing collections of life.

Life underwater deserves as much respect as life on land.

(3.8 l) of tap water. (Sea salts are preferred because although the brine shrimp will hatch in the table salt solution, they may not survive in it more than a week.)

3. Pour the salt water into the bowl and add a pinch of brine shrimp eggs. Some of the eggs will eventually sink to the bottom of the bowl. These have the best chance of hatching.

4. Place the bowl in a warm location. In a day or two, some of the shrimp should hatch. Once they do, move the bowl to a cooler spot.

## Observation

Use the magnifying glass to observe the baby brine shrimp, called nauplii (NAW-ply). Notice how they swim. What happens when you place a light next to the bowl?

Nauplii will turn into adult brine shrimp in about three weeks and start laying eggs of their own if conditions are right. To try raising them, first move the nauplii to a less salty solution. Then, add some warm water to a package of dry yeast and feed a few pieces of this mixture to the growing shrimp each day.

Brine shrimp are located near the bottom of the coral reef food chain, which means many creatures higher up the chain eat them for survival. Despite their size, brine shrimp, and even smaller animals called zooplankton, are indirectly responsible for the success of some of the reef's largest residents, such as the barracuda and moray eel.

# A CRYSTAL REEF

Although coral reefs are formed in the ocean over time by living creatures, you can watch a "reef" spring up quickly inside your home or classroom by setting off a few chemical reactions. Your model reef will be composed of crystals rather than limestone skeletons, but you will still be able to see how a whole colony can build upon the back of one individual.

First, place a handful of charcoal briquet pieces (about one by two inches [2.5 x 5 cm]) in a wide, deep bowl. In a separate bowl, mix six tablespoons (90 ml) of liquid laundry blueing with one or two tablespoons (15–30 ml) of water. Add six tablespoons (90 ml) of table salt and one tablespoon (15 ml) of ammonia. Pour the mixture over the charcoal.

Next, set the bowl of charcoal in a place where it won't be disturbed. In as little as an hour or two, you may see tiny crystals appear. Don't worry if your model reef takes longer; some are slower growers than others. Once the crystals start to form, sprinkle drops of food coloring on them to create your own colorful "coral reef."

## LEARN MORE ABOUT CORAL REEFS

The Coral Reef Alliance
2014 Shattuck Avenue
Berkeley, CA 94704
http://www.coral.org

Great Barrier Reef Marine Park Authority
2-68 Flinders Street
P.O. Box 1379
Townsville, Queensland 4810
Australia
http://www.gbrmpa.gov.au

Hawaii Coral Reef Network
(Online resource dedicated to coral reef
    conservation)
http://www.coralreefnetwork.com

The Reef Education Network
(Internet resource focused on coral reefs)
http://www.reef.edu.au

ReefKeeper International
2829 Bird Avenue, Suite 5, PMB 162
Miami, FL 33133
http://www.reefkeeper.org

U.S. Environmental Protection Agency
Office of Wetlands, Oceans, and Watersheds
    (4501 T)
1200 Pennsylvania Avenue, NW
Washington, D.C. 20460
http://www.epa.gov/owow/oceans/coral

## INDEX

Coral reefs provide homes for beautiful anemones.